W9-CZK-641

The Love Affair of
Mr. Ding and Mrs. Dong

Distributed to schools and libraries
in Canada by
SAUNDERS BOOK CO.
Box 308
Collingwood, Ontario, Canada L9Y 3Z7
(800) 461-9120

ISBN 089565-817-8
Library of Congress Cataloging-in-Publication Data
available upon request

The Love Affair

of Mr. Ding

and Mrs. Dong

author: Lionel Koechlin
illustrator: Annette Tamarkin Hatwell

The Child's World
Mankato, Minnesota

68.954

Mr. Ding is never willing to hurry.

As for Mrs. Dong, she is always trying to save time. Mr. Ding and Mrs. Dong live in the same town, but they don't know each other.

At mealtimes, Mr. Ding pecks at his lukewarm mashed potatoes. How slow he is!

As for Mrs. Dong, she just swallows down her
vegetables without cooking them.

At Easter, Mr. Ding goes down into his garden too late. His snail has already eaten up all the chocolate eggs.

At Easter, would you believe it, Mrs. Dong has already started decorating her Christmas tree.

In September, Mr. Ding is picking cherry pits. Too late, Mr. Ding!

In July, Mrs. Dong is looking for unripe
blackberries in the bramble bushes. Too early,
Mrs. Dong!

When Mr. Ding goes to see a funny movie, he bursts out laughing when the performance has been over for ages.

When Mrs. Dong goes to the circus, she applauds the juggler before his act is finished, and causes an accident.

Mr. Ding wants to go skiing. But by the time he gets to the top of the mountain, the snow has already melted away.

Mrs. Dong wants to go swimming. But when she gets to the beach, it's still low tide.

Mr. Ding drags his feet so much he wears his shoes out.

Mr. Ding takes his shoes to the best shoe repair
shop in town.

A year goes by. At last Mr. Ding decides to go and
pick up his shoes.

The same day, Mrs. Dong breaks the heels on both her shoes while she's having a race with the elevator.

The shoe repair man tells Mrs. Dong,
"Your shoes aren't ready yet. Wait for the
adhesive to dry."
The shoe repair man tells Mr. Ding,
"Your shoes are waiting for you in the attic. I'll go
up and get them."

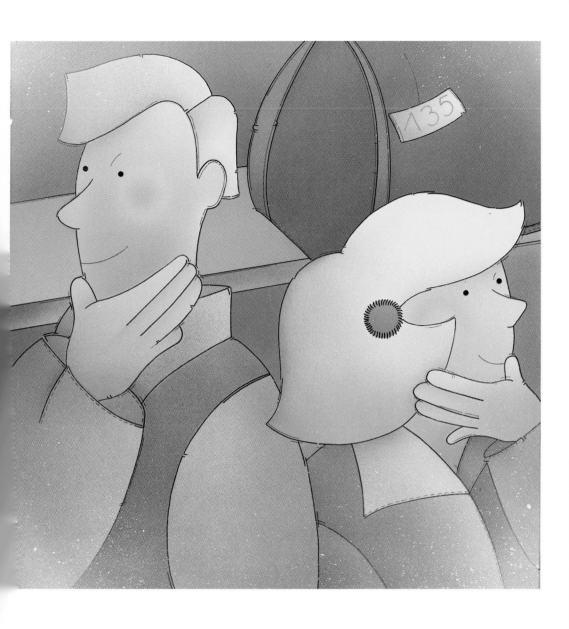

Mr. Ding is afraid he might stammer, and Mrs. Dong is afraid she might sputter.

Mr. Ding and Mrs. Dong listen to their two hearts beating together. "Ding Dong, Ding Dong, Ding Dong…"

Ding Dong, Ding…Mr. Ding slowly puts his hand on Mrs. Dong's hand. Ding Dong. Mrs. Dong pricks her cheek as she puts a kiss on Mr. Ding's cheek.

What a lovely wedding!

Ding Dong, Ding Dong. The zebra leads the
wedding party and on the bride's train, the snail
is fast asleep.

THE CHILD'S WORLD LIBRARY

A DAY AT HOME

A PAL FOR MARTIN

APARTMENT FOR RENT

CHARLOTTE AND LEO

THE CHILLY BEAR

THE CRYING CAT

THE HEN WITH THE WOODEN LEG

IF SOPHIE

JOURNEY IN A SHELL

KRUSTNKRUM!

THE LAZY BEAVER

LEONA DEVOURS BOOKS

THE LOVE AFFAIR OF MR. DING AND MRS. DONG

LULU AND THE ARTIST

THE MAGIC SHOES

THE NEXT BALCONY DOWN

OLD MR. BENNET'S CARROTS

THE RANGER SMOKES TOO MUCH

RIVER AT RISK

SCATTERBRAIN SAM

THE TALE OF THE KITE

TIM TIDIES UP

TOMORROW WILL BE A NICE DAY

THE TREE POACHERS